JAN 7 2002

P9-CCP-322

3 3089 00450 9075

Have You Ever Done That?

Have You Ever Done That?

JULIE LARIOS

Pictures by
ANNE HUNTER

Front Street
Asheville, North Carolina

WAUCONDA AREA LIBRARY
801 N. MAIN STREET
WAUCONDA, IL 60084

for John and Mary, and for Mom,
who read to us — JL

to Andrew —AH

Text copyright © 2001 by Julie Larios
Illustration copyright © 2001 by Anne Hunter
Printed in China
Designed by Helen Robinson
All rights reserved
First edition

Larios, Julie Hofstrand
Have you ever done that? / Julie Larios; illustrations by Anne Hunter.—1st ed.
p. cm.
ISBN 1-886910-49-9
1. Nature—Juvenile poetry. 2. Children's poetry, American.
[1. Nature—Poetry. 2. American poetry.] I. Hunter, Anne, ill. II. Title.

PS3562.A7233 H38 2001
811'.54—dc21   00-059326

Have you ever slept outside on a hot summer night?

Everything looks different
in the moon's strange light.
The trees seem to whisper
so you bravely whisper back.

Outside at night.
Have you ever done that?

I've never slept outside on a hot summer night
but I've ridden in a boat
    being tossed like a kite
        on dark wild waves
            with the wind at my back.

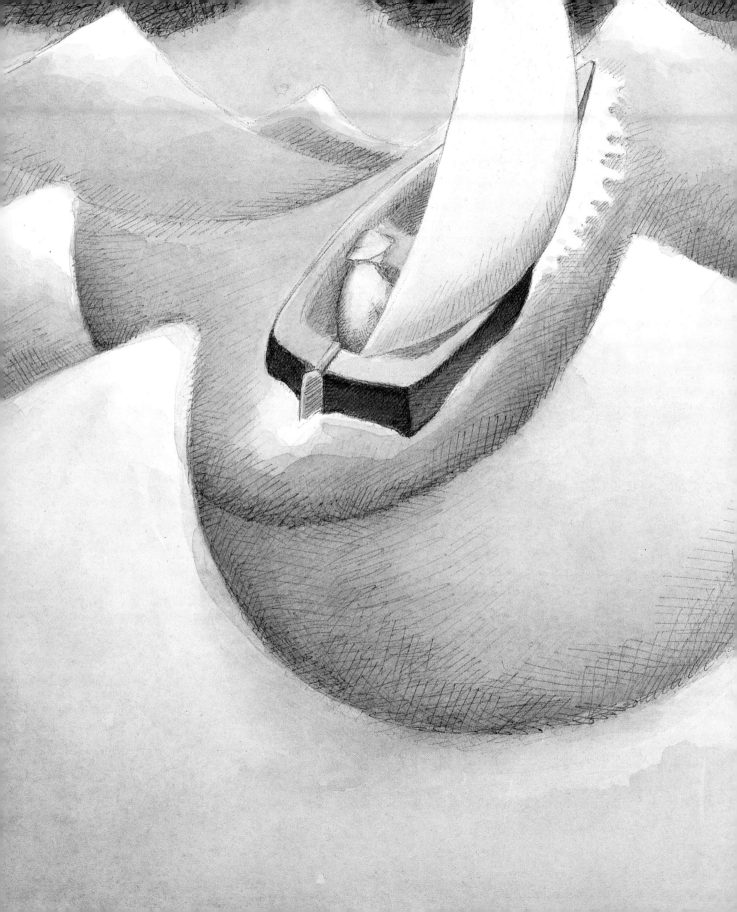

On a boat in a storm.

Have you ever done that?

I've never been tossed by the waves that way
but I've picked up a corn snake
sneaking its way
through still stalks of corn
growing ripe and fat.

Held a hungry snake.

Have you ever done that?

I've never held a snake with a meal on its mind
but I've nursed a baby crow
so I had to find
        potato bugs and hot worms
            and food from the cat.

Nursed a baby bird.
Have you ever done that?

I've never nursed a hurt bird to health, young or old,
but once I built some waxed paper wings
sprinkled gold

and I flew off the porch
to the lilac bush and back.

Flown with wings.

    Have you ever done that?

I've never built wings
    but once I flew out across the river
        on a rope
            and I knew that the water
                was deep and cold and black.

And I still let go.

Have you ever done that?

When the river is deep
　and the corn snakes pause,
　　when the wild waves call
　　　and the wounded crow caws,

Just stretch your wings
in the moon's strange light.

You can start by sleeping out on a hot summer night.